Whatcha Doing?

FOR MY
FOUR MOTHERS
NB

This IS
GENNY'S
BOOK
-AF

Whatcha Doing?

By Agatha Featherstone

Illustrated by Nicole Blau

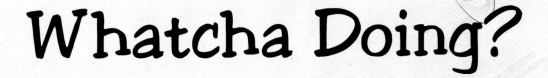

AZRO PRESS • SANTA FE, NEW MEXICO

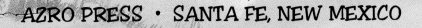

ISBN 1-929115-04-0
Library of Congress Card Number: 00-109865

Text © 2000 Azro Press
Illustrations © 2000 Nicole Blau

All rights reserved.
Design by Marcy Heller and Gae Eisenhardt
Text font is Jester 24 and 28 pt

Published in Santa Fe

Azro Press
PMB 342 • 1704 Llano St B
Santa Fe NM 87505
www.azropress.com

Printed in Thailand

Once upon a time,
a little boy asked. . .

Whatcha doing?

I'm planting potatoes.
Do you want to dig too?

Whatcha
doing?

I'm just lying here
reading and
enjoying the day.

Whatcha doing?

I'm feeding the cat.
Want to help?

Whatcha
doing?

I'm building a castle.
Want to put a block on the top?

Whatcha
doing?

I'm going to wash the dog.
Here, hold onto his collar for me.

Whatcha
doing?

I'm making cookies.
Would you like to
lick the bowl?

Whatcha
doing?

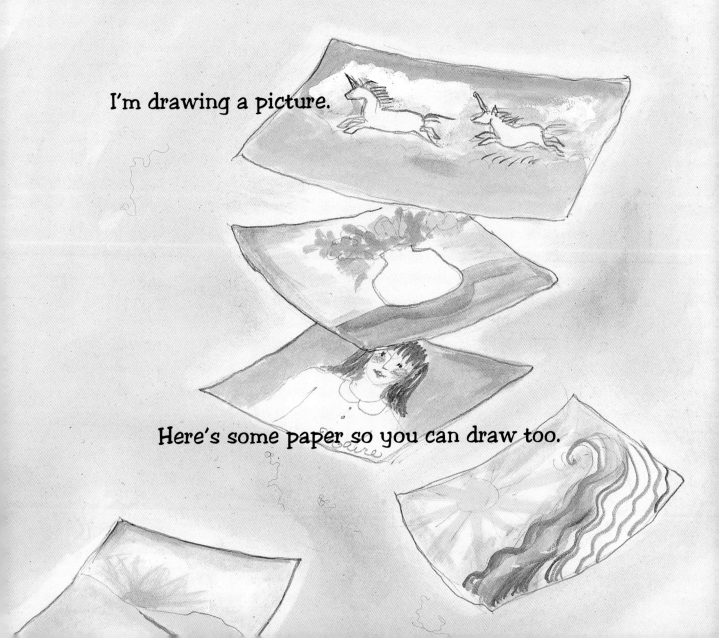

I'm drawing a picture.

Here's some paper so you can draw too.

Whatcha
doing?

I'm watching the game.
Do you want to
watch with me?

Whatcha doing?

I'm doing my homework.

You are so lucky! You don't have to go to school yet!

Whatcha
doing?

Going skating,
that's what.

Whatcha
doing?

I'm looking for
my glasses.
Have you seen them?

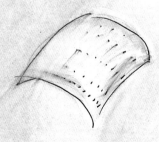

Whatcha
doing?

I'm washing
my hands.
Can you give me
that towel, please?

I'll show you how
to wash your hands
too, and then . . .

I'll read your book to you!